To Euan

Very best wishes

Margaret Isaac

TALES OF GOLD

Stories of Caves, Gold and Magic

Margaret Isaac

Illustrations by
Barbara Crow

APECS PRESS CAERLEON

Published by
APECS Press
Caerleon
Wales UK

© Margaret Isaac 2005
Reprinted 2010

Editing and design by
APECS Press Caerleon

ISBN 978 0 9563965 0 1

The publisher acknowledges the financial
support of the Welsh Books Council

Printed in Wales by Gwasg Dinefwr, Llandybie

For Alun

*and the little girl who
saw Elidyr walk into
the mound*

CONTENTS

BY THE SAME AUTHOR

Chwedlau A Diwylliant Cymru (1991): Storiau am Ogofâu, Aur, a Hud a Lledrith.

Nia and the Magic of the Lake (2000): The story of a growing friendship between a boy and a girl set in the first half of the 20th century, against the backdrop of the legend of the Lady of the Lake at Llyn-y-Fan Fach.

Sir Gawain and the Green Knight (2000): It is Christmas time in King Arthur's court. Gawain, Arthur's nephew accepts a mortal challenge from an enchanted giant.

Rhiannon's Way (2002): Caradog, a Celtic chieftain has been captured by the Romans. His daughter, Rhiannon sets out to rescue him with the help of her friend Brychan, and a little help from a magic pony and a magic mirror.

The Tale of Twm Siôn Cati (2005): The story of how a Welshman resisted the oppression of Tudor times on behalf of the poor in the same way as another Celtic hero, the Scottish outlaw, Rob Roy.

Lake Stories of Wales – Shadows in the Waters (2008): Stories based on the folklore associated with five lakes in South Wales.

Storïau Llynnoedd Cymru – Cysgodion yn y Dyfroedd (2008): Straeon wedi'u seilio ar chwedloniaeth pum llyn yn ne Cymru.

Thomas Jones of Tregaron alias Twm Siôn Cati (2009): Widely regarded as the Welsh outlaw known as Twm Siôn Cati, Thomas Jones lived during the reigns of five monarchs to become acknowledged as the greatest heraldic bard in Wales.

Teaching Story in the Primary School (1999):
Language resources for 4 – 7year olds based on the story, *The Owl Who Was Afraid of the Dark* by Jill Tomlinson.

Language Learning through Story (2000):
Language resources for 8 – 11year olds based on the story, *Owain Lawgoch and the Sleeping Knights* from *Tales of Gold* by Margaret Isaac.

Language Learning through Story (2000):
Language resources for 8 – 11year olds based on the story, *Nia and the Magic of the Lake* by Margaret Isaac.

Language Learning through Story (2000):
Language resources for 8 – 11year olds based on the story, *Sir Gawain and the Green Knight* by Margaret Isaac.

Language resources through story (2002):
Language resources for 8 – 11year olds based on the story, *Rhiannon's Way* by Margaret Isaac.

The following websites provide further useful information:

Apecs Press Caerleon: www.apecspress.com

Welsh Books Council: www.gwales.com

National Trust: www.nationaltrust.org.uk/main/w-dolaucothigoldmines

County Museum Carmarthen:
www.carmarthenshiremuseum.org.uk/history/index.html

FOREWORD

This collection of five traditional Welsh stories focuses on the acquisition and loss of gold and the appreciation that 'wealth' is more than a precious metal. It is a well researched text written specifically for the target audience. It has both literary and cultural merit with its south Wales geographical context of the Dolaucothi Gold Mines and Lampeter area connections and also has a universal moral resonance. The fascination of gold, 'sleeping' bloodthirsty knights, rural shepherds and drovers, and magician Merlin's quest for the elusive Philosopher's Stone, conjure up an intriguing, enjoyable anthology with plenty of food for thought.

Celtic-inspired ink drawings and borders both illustrate the narratives and provide a historical context, which is apt and stimulating and offer a model for young artists to explore and emulate.

Suitable as stand-alone tales, the stories are also cleverly related and linked to form a satisfying whole for those 8-11 year olds who decide to read them all in order.

More advanced readers will relish the style and sometimes challenging vocabulary in keeping with the genre, whilst all youngsters at Key Stage 2 will enjoy sharing these stories which would benefit from being read aloud. In a school setting, there is plenty of scope for drama and story telling, accepting that male characters are the norm here, a factor which might encourage reluctant boys, but not dissuade others.

The solid geographical context makes the text ideal for meeting requirements of the Curriculum Cymreig, providing scope for research and contemporary study, whilst the mystery and moral elements lend it to exploration and development of Thinking Skills.

This collection is a treasure which deserves to be in print and accessible to twenty-first century children and beyond.

The editor wishes to acknowledge the advice and assistance of the Welsh Books Council and Lorna Herbert Egan in relation to the above foreword.

BEFORE YOU BEGIN

Visit Pumpsaint, near Lampeter in South Wales and you will find the Dolaucothi Gold Mine. Long ago, many slaves from other countries worked in this mine digging for gold. Their Roman masters shipped the gold from the port at Caerleon and used it to help maintain the Roman Empire!

Throughout the ages, many have fought and died for gold in other countries all over the world, because gold has always been considered the most precious metal in the earth.

Others have searched in vain for the Philosopher's Stone which can change any metal into gold. This, they believed, would give them untold wealth and power.

Walk inside the goldmine at Dolaucothi and you will see crystals gleaming on the sides of the caves, crystals that look like sapphires and diamonds. The dragon, in the story called *The Dragon's Hoard,* flew off with a hoard of precious jewels across the night skies to try to protect it from humans. If you talk to old folk around Neath or Swansea, they will tell you that they have seen a dragon flying across the night sky, bearing this precious burden.

Visit the County Museum at Carmarthen and you will find a necklace made of gold. The gold used for the necklace came from the Dolaucothi Gold Mine. Perhaps it was part of the dragon's hoard.

Travel further along the valley and you will come to Carreg Cennen. This is where Owain Lawgoch is buried in a cave beneath the castle. Owain Lawgoch fought valiantly for the Welsh and the French against the English. He used his sword with such might and ferocity that they say his hand and arm was steeped in the blood of the enemy, that is why he was known as Owain Lawgoch, Owain of the Red Hand!

Visit the castle at Llandeilo and walk around the Dinefwr Estate. In the family churchyard, many gravestones bear the name of Urien, a knight of King Arthur. The lords of Dinefwr still bear the name of Urien.

Stand on the hills above the Dolaucothi Gold mine and look across the valley. You will see a mound. A little girl once told me that this was where Elidyr walked into his world of enchantment!

Listen to the golden harp of Huw and you will hear the tales as often as you wish....

Margaret Isaac

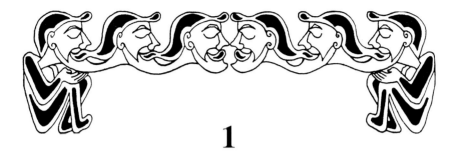

1

OWAIN LAWGOCH
and the Sleeping Knights

Long ago, when dragons roamed the land, in the time of wizards and witches, goblins and pixies, there lived a man named Huw'r Gollen (Huw of the Hazel Staff). He was a cattle drover. This was a hard life which required a strong, healthy man, used to living in the open air and capable of keeping his cattle fat and healthy on the long journey to market. The people of mid-Wales reared their cattle to sell to the rich, one of the favoured market places being London, where good business might be transacted.

At the time of our story, Huw's expedition had proved successful; true, two of the cows had died on the journey, and some had a little difficulty in the water of the ford at Aust, but he had negotiated a good price for the rest of the herd in the London market.

On his way home, as he was crossing London Bridge, he was stopped by a strange old man. His beard was long and flowing, wisps of white hair fell to his shoulders, his eyes were small and bright, nose prominent. He wore a long deep purple cloak, clasped at the shoulder by an elaborately carved gold brooch.

"Good day to you sir," he addressed Huw. "I see by that stout hazel staff you carry that you are a stranger here. Where might your homeland be?" "I come from Wales," replied Huw, "I am returning home after taking some cattle to London."

The old man drew closer to Huw and began speaking in low, urgent tones.

"Your hazel staff interests me greatly; if you could direct me to the tree from which it was cut, I could show you wealth beyond your wildest dreams."

Huw was astonished by the strange man's request but, being very inquisitive, he was also greatly intrigued. What man would not be enticed by this promise of riches and, perhaps, an exciting adventure.

"Sir," replied Huw, "I can take you to the very spot where the hazel tree grows and you may then show me what marvels you can."

The two men began the long and arduous journey, retracing their steps through the ford at Aust. Huw left the main road, striking across country, along hard and dusty tracks, through quagmires and treacherous rocky slopes. They skirted impenetrable forests and clambered over rugged outcrops until they reached a vast expanse of wild moorland.

They stumbled over the rough terrain until Huw paused and looked towards the East. He pointed to the horizon, and the wizard discerned a large grassy mound, sometimes called a barrow. As they approached he saw that at the side of the barrow grew a single hazel tree.

"This is the bush," said Huw, "I use it because it is strong and supple and grows at a prodigious rate."

The old man was silent, but his eyes gleamed, cunning and bright.

First, the wizard carefully peeled the bark from a small branch of the tree and concealed it in the folds of his cloak, then he walked right round the base of the tree, looking intently at the ground. At last he gave a grunt of triumph and, kneeling, he began scraping away the soil to reveal a large metal ring.

"Help me to clear away the earth around this ring," he growled to Huw.

The two men worked swiftly and silently, and soon revealed a slab of stone. They both took hold of the metal ring and pulled hard. Slowly, very slowly, the stone was raised until Huw found himself gazing down a succession of stone steps, descending into the bowels of the earth! The wizard led Huw down the steps into a dark, musty underground passage. As they made their way carefully along, they passed a large bell, hanging from the lichen-covered roof. They continued on their way until Huw became aware of a glowing light in the distance which became brighter as they approached until at last they reached the end of the tunnel and then, the sight which met Huw's eyes astounded him!

He found himself in an immense cave, in the centre of which was a gigantic stone table. A giant of a man, in full armour and wearing a crown of gold sat at the table, his hand resting on a huge sword of gleaming gold encrusted with rubies and diamonds – the hand was blood red! Twelve knights lay on the floor of the cave, seven lay with their feet towards the entrance and their heads towards the West, three others lay with their heads facing to the South, two others of great size lay ten yards further on, also with their heads facing South. They all lay with their faces turned upwards, their heads resting on their breasts with a ledge of rock acting as a pillow, for, the remarkable thing about the twelve knights and their royal leader was that they all lay in deepest slumber.

When Huw had taken in this amazing scene, he saw from whence the light came. Also on the floor of the cave, at the foot of the stone table, lay two heaps of shining metal coins. One heap shone gold, the other silver. Huw judged them to be about two metres high – it was the most marvellous sight he had ever experienced.

5

"The royal knight is Owain Lawgoch," whispered the wizard. "He and his knights are to sleep until Wales has need of them. You may take what treasure you are able to carry, but take care that you do not touch the large bell you saw in the tunnel. If you do cause it to ring, the knight will awake and ask 'Does Wales need us?' You must then reply, 'No, sleep thou on.'"

Huw noted what the wizard said, and gathering up as much gold as he could carry, he retraced his steps, carefully avoiding the bell, until he reached the surface once more.

Huw was now a wealthy man, and enjoyed great popularity among his friends. But, sad to say, he squandered his wealth and found himself a poor man once more. Why should he worry? He knew of an unlimited source of wealth.

He returned to the grassy mound and the hazel tree, easily locating the slab of stone, the passageway and the cavern of treasure. However, in his haste to

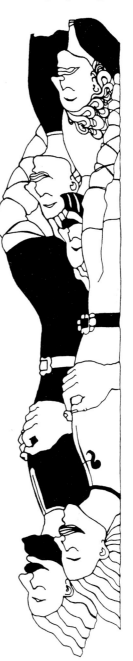

get away with rather more than he could carry, he accidentally knocked the bell and its sonorous tone rang ominously along the passage, re-echoing around the cavern.

Owain Lawgoch raised his head, eyes open wide and said: "Does Wales need us?" Huw remembered the reply: "No, sleep thou on," and the knight fell at once into his slumber.

Time passed, and Huw once more needed gold. Returning to the hazel tree and the cave, he thought, "This time I don't see why I should not take as much as I can carry from both heaps of treasure." He had become greedy with the wealth he could acquire with such ease.

He reached the cave and began filling two sacks, one with gold coins and one with silver. He staggered back along the passage, barely able to carry his heavy burden. He was so overladen, he inevitably bumped against the great bell which rang even more loudly and ominously than the first time. Owain Lawgoch, fully awake, demanded: "Does Wales need us?"

Huw, utterly afraid, found that he had forgotten the reply. As he stood, tongue tied and terrified, all the knights stood up and joined their ferocious leader.

They looked threateningly at poor Huw, as Owain Lawgoch roared: "This pathetic creature deserves the direst punishment, he has defiled the treasure of the people of Wales. Take him, my valiant knights, and cast him out."

They bore down on Huw, who felt himself rushed along as if he were borne aloft on a whirlwind. He was hurled through the tunnel and felt himself flung on the turf above the ground. Lying dazed, with his eyes closed, he realised he had lost his gold, his silver and his hazel staff. He sat up and looked around him. The mound and the tree had completely vanished. Bruised and sore, he limped home, sadder and wiser than before.

Huw lived on for many years, no longer as a cattle drover, for he had lost his former strength, but as a menial servant to a wealthy landowner. Thus was Owain Lawgoch's prediction fulfilled. Many times Huw searched for the hazel tree, the mound and the cave, but he never found them again.

The wizard was, of course, Merlin. As many people know, the hazel has magic properties and Merlin had required that particular hazel bark for a special purpose. What that purpose was and what happened to Merlin is, however, another story.

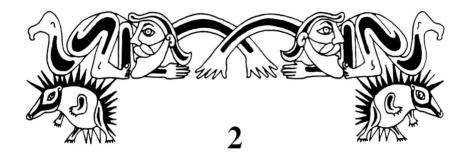

2

FOOL'S GOLD

Dewi Rhys was a shepherd who lived near some old gold mines in Wales. He loved his work, looking after the sheep and climbing the beautiful hills around his home. He sometimes walked along the banks of the river, watching the fish jumping, or strolled among the trees along the mountainside, watching the birds soaring high in a cloudless sky, while the sheep munched the sweet grass. Occasionally he spotted a hedgehog scuttling away into the undergrowth.

One cold bright February morning, Dewi was not in his customary happy mood. In the morning, at breakfast time, his wife had asked him for money to buy food, and had reminded him that the children needed new clothes. But he had no money to give her. As he climbed the hills, he felt very unhappy, because they were so very poor. He loved his family dearly, but oh! how he wished that he could hit upon some good luck and be a rich man instead of a poor shepherd.

As he climbed over a stile and jumped to the ground, he noticed a hedgehog, behaving very strangely. Instead of scuttling into the undergrowth at the approach of a human, it kept looking up at Dewi, snuffling along in front of him and strangest of all, placing its small hand in front of its snout and winking its eye.

Dewi was fascinated, and began to follow the strange creature as it made its way to the river bank. The hedgehog stopped by a stone at the side of the river, it waited expectantly, Dewi was curious and went to the stone, lifted it and looked underneath.

To his astonishment, he found a bright gold coin. He was delighted at his good luck and quickly put the gold coin in his pocket. He didn't notice that the strange hedgehog was changing its shape. Its feet and legs began to look almost human, its prickles became

softer and lighter until they became soft hairs, and the hedgehog seemed to be half like a child and half like an old man of eighty! The hedgehog-goblin disappeared quietly into the bushes.

Dewi hurried home with his new gold coin safely tucked in his pocket. He carefully placed his treasure in a wooden box which he kept in his bedroom.

The following morning, as Dewi went about his work with his sheep, he thought about his adventure of the previous day. Curiosity drew him to the place by the river where he had found his gold coin under a stone. To his surprise, the stone was in the same place. Of course, Dewi could not resist lifting it, to look underneath and to his surprise, he found another gold coin. He hurried home and placed the second gold coin in his wooden box in his bedroom.

He was very pleased to think that he was a little richer with his two gold coins, and he wondered if he might find a gold coin beneath the stone every day. He might then become a very rich man indeed. And of course this is what he did. Every day, on his way to work, he went to the stone by the river, lifted

it up and always found a gold coin. Soon his wooden box in his bedroom was quite full.

Unfortunately, he didn't notice that as he was going down to the stone by the river every day, a stranger had begun to follow him, watching him as he bent down over the stone by the river, and he saw Dewi pick up a gold coin and put it in his pocket.

Dewi did not know about the stranger, and you might think that he was now very happy with his new found riches, but sad to say, Dewi had become quite mean, and did not want to part with his gold coins. He liked to keep them in the wooden box and count them every night before he went to bed. So when his wife asked him for money for food or for the children's clothes, he pretended he didn't have any.

One morning, weeks later, he woke in an unusually bad temper, quarrelled with his wife and scolded his children. He went to work feeling very unhappy. "Oh well," he thought, "I can get my gold coin from the stone by the river. At least, I am making myself richer every day." But the thought did not comfort him as much as it used to do.

As he made his way along the usual path to the river bank, he saw a strange man bending down, lifting the stone and looking underneath. The stranger put something in his pocket and began to hurry away. Dewi ran after him, but before he could catch him up, the man had disappeared amongst the trees.

Dewi rose very early the next morning, meaning to get to the stone first, so that the stranger would not get the gold coin before him. He hurried quickly to the place by the river bank, lifted the stone and, to his great dismay, he found nothing underneath but a heap of red dust! What he failed to notice was the hedgehog-goblin watching silently from the bracken.

On his way home, Dewi comforted himself. "At least I have the money I have saved in my wooden box," he thought.

He climbed the stairs to his bedroom and pulled the box out from beneath his bed. He opened the lid and what do you think he found? No gold coins, only a heap of red dust. Dewi was angry and confused. He was very angry because he no longer had his gold coins, he quarrelled with his wife, and once again, was bad-tempered with his children. A blight was cast over his home and his children were sad and silent. They were all very unhappy that their once loving father had become such a bad-tempered man.

Some weeks later, Dewi was out in the hills as usual, and happened to pass the spot by the river, where he had first encountered the hedgehog-goblin. He heard very weird chanting coming from some bushes nearby.

He crept up and carefully pulled the bushes aside. He was astonished and frightened to see the hedgehog-goblin dancing in a circle with other goblins just like himself.

This is what the goblin sang:

> My spell is cast, my way at last
> is clear for all to see,
> Tonight I come to human house
> A human child I'll seem.

Dewi was horrified. He knew of tales of fairy folk and goblins who wanted to change places with humans and live in the human world. They might pretend to look like the person they had changed places with, except that they would behave in odd ways. People called such creatures, changelings.

"This is not going to happen in my house," vowed Dewi. "I am sure that this hedgehog-goblin thought it might have a better chance to become a changeling in my home, because I was making my family so unhappy. I have been behaving very badly, but now I know what to do, to make sure that I keep my children safe."

Dewi went upstairs, took out his wooden box and burned it. Then he went to the church, and prayed for forgiveness for his bad temper and his greed, and asked God to help him to protect his children. He took some holy water from the church and carried it back to his home. He sprinkled it everywhere in the house, but especially where his children slept.

That night, Dewi stayed awake all night, keeping watch over his children's beds, but he need not have worried. Had he looked out of the window, he would have seen nothing but the stars in the sky, the shadows on the mountains and a hedgehog snuffling away in the undergrowth.

3

ELIDYR

Elidyr felt angry. He scuffed the ground moodily, not noticing the golden sunlight glinting through the trees. He loved his mother and was uncomfortable about the way he had treated her. But he was angry at the way she had treated him. The morning had begun well, with Elidyr waking to the sound of the house martins chirruping loudly as the young tried out their wings. It was the nest that had caused the problems.

The boy had not meant to destroy it; he loved watching the parent birds swooping, slicing, prodding food into the everlasting ever-open beaks. When the young ones emerged from the nest, teetering on spindled toes, nervously imitating their parents' more graceful flight, Elidyr had wanted to see the nest close up.

What followed was an accident. He had lost his footing from the stool and, grabbing at the plank of wood to break his fall, he had instead pulled the nest from its mooring, and brought it to the ground where it lay in fragments of mud and straw on the barn floor. His mother had been unreasonable in blaming him for the death of the birds. He had not seen the cat until it was too late. In a moment the birds were dead.

He shut his eyes miserably and pressed his small body against the tree trunk. So he did not see a small creature standing near his foot, he only heard a strange rustling which caused him to open his eyes and look down. Surprised and frightened, he saw a boy, like himself, with fair hair, blue eyes, well proportioned limbs, and wearing identical clothes, only, the boy he was looking at was no bigger than a baby hedgehog. Elidyr was hypnotised as the creature laid his finger on his lips, pointed toward the distant hills and beckoned to Elidyr to follow him. Mesmerised, Elidyr obeyed, and as they crept silently through the forest, he heard the rustling increase and saw that they had been joined by a throng of small people. Apart from their size, they looked much like the people Elidyr lived amongst in his normal life.

Elidyr was led out of the forest, down a winding road, over rough moorland where the ground became very rocky, until they were climbing over crags and outcrops and came to rest in front of a smooth green mound. The little people surrounded Elidyr in silence while his first companion advanced towards the mound. He walked on and on and – disappeared!

Elidyr, pulled along by his companions, was encouraged to do the same. He found that he too was able to walk through the mound as if he had been made of air!

As he passed through to the other side, he became aware of strange sounds, beautiful tinkling music, silvery laughter. He was walking along a dark underground passage but could see a glow ahead. The glow became a brighter and brighter light until his eyes became quite dazzled.

When Elidyr became accustomed to the brightness, the sight which met his eyes astounded him. The room was semi-circular in shape, large and warm. The uneven walls shone with gold and crystal and swept upwards to a high ceiling encrusted with diamonds, pearls and rubies, laced with gold. The floor, of dull gold, was overlaid with a deep, rich carpet, cunningly woven with emblems of dragons, serpents and other strange beasts. In the centre of the room, a cauldron of gold, gave forth a mouth-watering smell of every delicious food Elidyr could imagine. The finest cooked fish, baked meats, fruits and sweet delicacies, all seemed contained in one vessel.

A round table covered with a cloth of gold was surrounded by exquisitely carved golden chairs. The cloth of gold was embroidered with fine silks of every hue. Plates and goblets of gold encrusted with rubies and sapphires were placed on this fine table. Elidyr was led to the table by his new companions. While his feet were bathed and his hair was combed,

he was served with the most nourishing and tempting meal of his life. To his astonishment, the cauldron remained full, a source of everlasting sustenance.

As his plate was filled, so he ate from a golden dish and drank from a burnished goblet and found that whatever he consumed, was a delight to taste as he had never tasted before. He forgot his mother, his family and his friends from the other world. He felt happiness well up inside him like a warm wave flowing through him, enveloping him in a rosy cloud of bliss. A harp of gold played golden music which made him dream of bubbling merry streams, velvet green meadows and warm purple mountains.

He was given many playthings, but his favourite was a golden ball. The games he played were of great variety and he never grew tired of this favourite amusement. When he wished to rest, the golden ball would entrance him with delightful pictures as he gazed into its glowing centre. Thus Elidyr was happy for many years in the land beyond the mountains in his cavern of gold.

One day, as he lay outstretched gazing intently into the golden ball, he saw, within the picture, a figure he dimly recognised. He closed his eyes to remember and thought for the first time of his mother and, for the first time, tears came to his eyes. He begged his fairy companions to let him return home for a short while, to visit his mother. After much hesitation, for they loved him dearly, the fairy folk consented.

They led him along the passage, took him by the hand and gently drew him through the cave and into the outside world.

He left them and ran joyously along remembered paths, down, down, to the home in which he had once lived. Suddenly, he stopped, for he could see his mother, outside their small dwelling, gathering wood for the hearth. He raced towards her and flung himself into her arms. "Elidyr, my son," she looked surprised, "don't take on so, you couldn't prevent a cat from killing birds." Elidyr stood frozen. That had happened long ago – years ago! "Come along," she said, "It's time you had some tea."

He tried to tell his mother of his great adventure he told her of the fairy folk, the cave, the wondrous gold and jewels, the golden ball.

However much he insisted, she could not believe him, she merely thought he was over-imaginative. "If what you tell me is true," she said, "bring me but the golden ball which you love so dearly. That will be not only a proof, but will provide the riches we need to give us comfort for ever."

Elidyr was worried. He had found happiness in the hollow behind the hills and did not like to betray a trust. But he loved his mother dearly and hated to think of her hands becoming calloused and rough-red with hard work, of her dear face becoming worn and her body wasting with poverty and disease. "I shall have to steal the golden ball and thereby steal some happiness for my mother."

Elidyr was approaching the place where he had first met his small companion. The fairy folk silently reappeared, from the ground, from the flowers, the grass, the stones. They led him once more to their home and all entered the mountain.

Inside the cave, Elidyr was once more fed, clothed and entertained with entrancing music. At last he was left alone, clasping his beloved golden ball. His companions, fast asleep, trusted him as a friend.

Gathering his courage, Elidyr, clutching his golden ball, began to retrace his steps along the underground passage.

He carefully stepped over the sleeping figures, the sleeping animals, the sleeping stones. He stepped through the mountain and began to run down the hillside toward his home. A great shout stopped him. It came from all the fairy folk who had suddenly surrounded him. Their King furiously upbraided Elidyr, calling him a thief and a traitor.

Then, as suddenly, everyone vanished. Elidyr looked into his hands, they were empty, the golden ball had disappeared. He looked back at the hills, they looked the same, brooding, mysterious, but the well-known path to the cave had gone.

Elidyr sadly retraced his steps homeward. He and his mother lived together for many years until eventually he took a wife. Sometimes, when the sunlight glinted golden through the trees, he thought he glimpsed something more – a small figure? a golden cauldron? a burnished chair? a golden ball?

But he never found his world of treasure again.

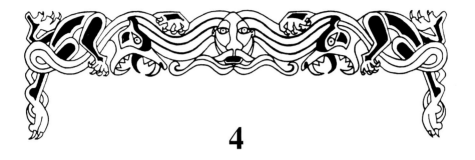

4

THE DRAGON'S HOARD

The sky was heavy with louring grey clouds that threatened a heavy downpour of rain. A rushing, roaring torrent of swirling waters from the river Tywi, an outward sign of the deluge that had already saturated the land around Llandeilo, frothed and foamed angrily at the foot of Dinefwr Castle. Sturdy oaks had been torn from the roots by the recent hurricane, the debris of branches and leaves lay scattered throughout the castle woods. The devastation stretched from Dinefwr across the Tywi River to the land in the North around Pumpsaint.

Merlin knew there was a very good reason for the unusual weather; the dragon was rumbling his displeasure in his new home, deep in the bowels of the earth. Vapour rising from the woods, mists shrouding the turrets of Dinefwr and Carreg Cennen were unmistakable signs of the fire-breathing dragon sulking in the dim recesses of his cavern. He had been forced to seek a new refuge for his precious hoard, since Merlin had located his previous hiding place.

Merlin had sighted him once more flying high in a dark blue, starlit sky, his scales glistening with the myriad colours given off by the gems he carried. The jewels and precious stones he bore were unbelievably beautiful to behold. His huge body and wings shone with sapphires, emerald, coral, amber and jade, while his long serpentine tail glistened with garnet, topaz and gold. This astonishing sight might stir the hearts of ordinary people, but Merlin was seeking a much richer prize.

His quest was more important and if successful, could change the lives of people everywhere in the world, for Merlin was in search of the Philosopher's Stone. As many people know, this stone had a magic property, it could turn any metal into gold. Think of it! Scientists could take any of the more commonly occurring ores, such as lead or copper, and, with the help of this stone, they could turn these ordinary metals into pure gold!

Many alchemists and scientists had spent a lifetime on this quest which was more hazardous than one might imagine. The search could only be conducted by a person with knowledge, perseverance and purity of heart. It also required great courage and ingenuity. Merlin was such a man, and had pursued this quest for many years.

He had already acquired some of the properties necessary to create the special stone, one of these had been the bark of a particular hazel tree he had obtained with the help of a cattle drover. But he believed that the one remaining element he needed to perfect his invention was — dragon's blood!

Merlin's cave was well hidden near a small place called Cil-y-Wain, three miles north of Dinefwr. He had located the dragon's lair near a lake called Llyn

Taliaris. The wizard had meditated long in preparing his plan to secure the dragon's blood as the final element to perfect his invention, the Philosopher's Stone. His eyes gleamed and his heart jumped when he thought of his triumph. Merlin, the wizard, the prophet, would be remembered for ever as the wisest and cleverest of men!

He had concocted a potion which would render the dragon harmless and enable him to obtain the precious dragon's blood; but he had two more deeds to accomplish. First, he had to find out more about the dragon's cave and the treasure, then, he had to enlist the aid of a brave knight. He knew the man who could give him the help he needed. His name was Urien, Lord of Dinefwr Castle, he was a cousin of King Arthur, and was renowned as a fierce warrior and a man of action.

Merlin set out on his expedition to the dragon's latest place of refuge, deep in the forest of Taliaris. The wizard journeyed at dead of night from Cil-y-Wain toward Maescastell. Nearing the lake, with his great magic, he changed his shape to one which would disguise him from the monster and enable him to enter the cave and explore the dragon's lair in safety.

The dragon, lay uneasy in slumber, and did not notice the slight whirring of wings as a small bee landed on a ledge of quartz rock near the dragon's wing. Merlin had chosen a clever disguise. As a bee, he was small enough to remain undetected by the dragon, but his large bee's eye could absorb every aspect of the scene which now met his gaze.

Merlin had expected a spectacular hoard of treasure, but the sight that met his eyes exceeded even his powerful imagination. Gems glinted and gleamed from the roof of the cavern, garnets, sapphires, rubies and diamonds embellished the smooth, glistening surfaces which formed the walls of the cave.

As Merlin's gaze came to rest on the gigantic bulk of the slumbering dragon, he spied the dull yellow lustre of gold beneath the monster's foot. Daringly, for Merlin could not resist looking more closely, he flew a little closer and saw the most intricately carved ornaments, among them a curious snake-shaped bracelet and a cunningly wrought necklet in the shape of a wheel.

This magnificent jewellery had been worn by Romans and Celts more than 1200 years earlier, and

Merlin now understood why the dragon took such care to hide and guard his priceless hoard. The bee whirred silently from the cave, along the passageway and out into the still night.

A huddle of silent black ravens perched in the trees above Dinefwr Castle as Merlin rapped impatiently at the gate. He had resumed his normal imposing presence, and a sleepy, bewildered porter recognized the wizard at once, with his piercing eyes, and his tall majestic figure, and instantly admitted him into the castle. Urien received him courteously and the gallant knight listened respectfully as Merlin told him of the dragon and his hoard of treasure. The good prince realized that gaining such wealth could be used to help the poor people of Dinefwr and readily agreed to help Merlin in the venture.

However, Merlin was a little more cunning than his new found friend, and thought it best to keep secret his true purpose in braving the dragon's lair, which was to obtain the monster's blood! Perhaps he was afraid that Urien would not be prepared to take part in an adventure for what he might regard as nothing more than a magician's fancy, after all, who would believe that a stone could be created that would turn any metal into gold!

Neither of the two men noticed the shadowy figure of a tall, beautiful woman slinking behind one of the great stone pillars as they talked together. They would have felt some alarm had they done so, for the figure was none other than that of the great enchantress Morgan le Fay, cousin of King Arthur. She was his sworn enemy, and was always on the look out for any means to bring disgrace or death to him and his valiant knights. She had discovered Merlin's plans by means of her own dark magic and had planned her own mischief to thwart him and Urien, who was one of Arthur's best loved knights.

Merlin and Urien set off for Taliaris on an uncomfortable and hazardous journey. They toiled through marshland and over inhospitable craggy rocks, unaware of the fleeting figure of Morgan Le Fay flitting across the plains and through the forest.

As the two men reached the mouth of the cave, Merlin gave Urien the lethal potion which would render the monster harmless, while Urien obtained the treasure. Merlin intended to extract a phial of the dragon's blood from his body, while Urien was collecting the gold and jewels, which would enable him to help his people.

Silently, they entered the cave, stepping carefully along the rough floor, they waded through deep pools as water dripped from the roof and seeped uncomfortably into their skin. They penetrated deeper into the darkness of the cavern until they reached the innermost chamber where the dragon lay.

As their eyes became accustomed to the darkness, they tried to make out the great bulk of the dragon, but to their dismay, they saw no monster as they expected, and no treasure. All that met their gaze was a high chamber, rough walls, a damp, dripping roof, and dark, dangerous-looking recesses. The huge bulk of the creature with his spectacular hoard of wealth was nowhere to be seen!

Urien was perplexed and looked at his friend in dismay. But Merlin stood deep in thought. He knew some great power was needed to foil his plan and in his great wisdom, he realized that the only creature capable of such mischief-making would be Morgan le Fay, and he knew of course that she hated anyone connected with her arch enemy King Arthur.

"Morgan le Fay must have discovered my plans and warned the dragon," he thought. "I shall have to find another way to obtain the one elusive ingredient – a dragon's blood – which I need to fulfil my dream of creating the Philosopher's Stone."

Aloud he said:

"The creature must have awoken and fled to another hiding place to avoid losing his precious treasure. It is the way of dragons, they constantly move from place to place to guard their gold and keep it safe from humans."

Urien was disappointed at the outcome of his adventure. He had hoped to improve the lot of his people, but he vowed that he would find other means to improve their way of life, and he was a resolute man and a good leader.

Disconsolately, the two men began to retrace their steps, but the eagle-eyed wizard saw something glimmering in a crack in the rocks alongside them. He gently extricated the object and cleaned it carefully and quietly with his voluminous sleeve. Holding it up to examine his find, he saw that it was a small, exquisitely carved Celtic harp made of pure gold. Carefully, he placed it in one of his many capacious pockets. Urien had not noticed the magician's surreptitious behaviour, he was ahead of the wizard, lost in his own thoughts.

The two men continued along the passageway and eventually emerged from the cave into the darkness of the night.

As they approached Dinefwr Castle, an unnatural light illuminated the sky. Looking up, they saw the dragon, slowly beating its wings, its body glittering with the priceless gems. It was heading North, in the direction of Talley Abbey and Pumpsaint.

So, the Philosopher's Stone remained a dream, a prize for the cleverest and wisest of men. Merlin still cherished the hope that one day he might be that man.

As for the gold harp, Merlin kept it in a secret place in his own cave. He prophesied that the other gold jewellery the dragon guarded so jealously would not be found for another 600 years. His prediction was fulfilled and some of these beautiful ornaments may now be seen in the County Museum, Carmarthen.

5

THE GOLDEN HARP

Merlin fingered the harp pensively and thought of the cattle drover who had led him to the cave of Owain Lawgoch many years before. As his fingers stirred idly across the strings, the wondrous tales of the Mabinogion stirred his imagination. Blodeuwedd, the woman Gwydion made out of flowers, Rhiannon and her prince, the dream of

Rhonabwy, all these beautiful stories were sung once more, through the golden notes of the enchanted harp which Merlin now held in his hands.

The harp was made of pure gold, embellished with sapphires and emeralds, while the strings were made of finest spun gold. Merlin knew that whoever possessed the harp would have the gift of music and poetry, and his thoughts turned once more to Huw the cattle drover. Through him, Merlin had obtained the hazel bark he had required in his search for the Philosopher's Stone, and the wizard felt some remorse, that Huw had suffered as a result of the adventure.

Huw was now working as a servant at Dinefwr Castle and often felt bitter with his lot, although his own greed had brought about his misfortune. Nevertheless, Merlin felt some responsibility for his guiding him to the treasure in the first place and resolved to make a gift of the golden harp to him.

Merlin journeyed from his cave to the castle and was admitted at once by the porter. The awe in which the wise Merlin was held by the people gave him easy access to any house in the land. He made his way to the servants' quarters and found Huw toiling in the kitchen. He looked up and at once recognised the wizard.

"Leave me be," Huw said unhappily, "your guile and cunning led me to this sad state, I want no more of your enchantment."

"Your present misfortune was brought upon you by your own greed," replied the wise Merlin. "Had you been satisfied with the treasure you obtained on your first visit to the cave, you might still be a happy man. However, I have not come to cause you further distress, I wish to help you."

Merlin led Huw out into the courtyard and both men sat down by the old well.

"You know that the people of Wales love to hear the old tales and that the minstrel is gladly received in the finest houses in the land. I can bestow upon you the gift of music and poetry, if you so wish, so that you would occupy a happier position than the one you now endure."

Huw listened with growing pleasure for he always loved listening to the old stories and had tried to remember them with only partial success.

"I would indeed be more than content if I could once more wander through my beloved land giving joy to others through tales I sang", replied Huw, "but how can you do this thing for me?"

"Here is a golden harp," replied Merlin, "I took it from an enchanted cave. Whoever owns it will possess the gift of music and poetry."

Merlin handed the harp to Huw, who took it, tremulously at first. He held it lovingly in his hands and felt the warm smooth gold beneath his fingers. Gently, he plucked the enchanted strings and felt the power of the music stir his senses. He began to sing and the people of the castle, hearing the melodic tones, were drawn to listen. He sang of Culhwch and

Olwen, Peredur, the Lady of the Fountain and many more. The music ceased and Huw and the listeners seemed to wake as from a dream.

Huw was no longer the poor servant of the castle, he would now travel freely across the land, welcome in every household, singing his entrancing tales, and known henceforth as Huw y Delyn Aur – Huw of the Golden Harp.

Margaret Isaac was born in the Rhymney Valley, and was educated at the University of Wales, Cardiff. She writes for readers of all ages, her work being inspired by Celtic/Welsh legend. Tales of Gold is her first book in the present series.

She has a lifelong interest in Welsh legend and culture. The stories, Tales of Gold, were drawn from her work on the Dolaucothi Education Project, 1989-1992, which was the subject of a tripartite research study incorporating The National Trust, Gwent College and the University of Wales, Cardiff and Lampeter.

Barbara Crow was educated at the Slade School of Fine Art, Bristol and the University of Wales, Aberystwyth. She has illustrated for numerous publishers including Heinemann, Thames and Hudson, and Oxford University Press.